Disney's
Winnie the Pooh
Always Tell the Truth

It's easier to tell the truth

Than try to run away.

So take a breath

And speak right up,

And then go out and play!

"Woo-hoo-hoo!" Roo shouted, bouncing happily after Tigger. He and Tigger had already bounced through Rabbit's garden and Piglet's leaves and Eeyore's thistles.

"Whaddya say we visit our ol' pal Owl?" Tigger suggested.

"I'm ready when you are!" Roo exclaimed.
Roo followed his friend up to Owl's front door.

"I say," Owl greeted them, "what good timing! I just received a gift from Great-Aunt Cuthbert. I was hoping someone would stop by to see it!"

"What is it?" asked Tigger.

"The Owl Family *Who's Who* stool," Owl answered. "My great-grandfather started the *Who's Who* of Owls. He stepped upon this stool each fall to read the names of owls who had done great deeds that year."

"It looks kind of old," said Roo.

"Oh, my, yes, Roo!" Owl laughed. "So I must ask that it be off-limits for bouncing. Why, this stool dates back to . . . well, let me just check." Owl pulled out an old family album.

As Owl looked through his book, Tigger looked out the
window. "Say," Tigger said, "there's Pooh!"

"Where?" asked Roo. Without thinking, Roo bounced onto
the *Who's Who* stool. One of the legs cracked!

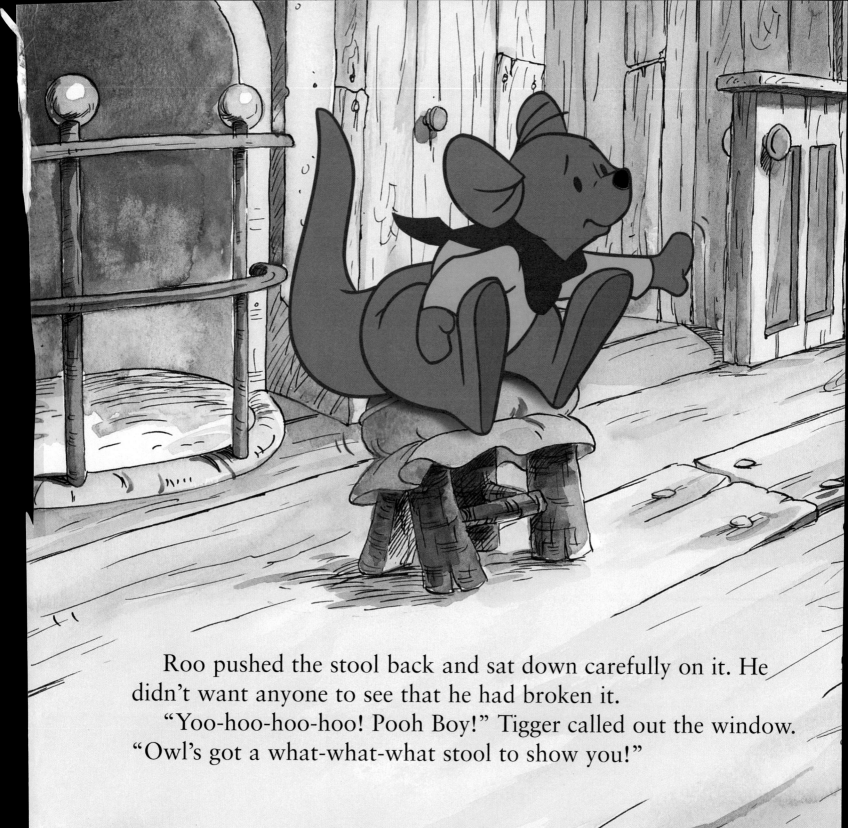

Roo pushed the stool back and sat down carefully on it. He didn't want anyone to see that he had broken it.

"Yoo-hoo-hoo-hoo! Pooh Boy!" Tigger called out the window. "Owl's got a what-what-what stool to show you!"

"Tigger!" Roo whispered. "I need your help!"

"What's the problem, Little Buddy?" Tigger asked.

Roo showed Tigger the broken stool leg. "I have to fix it before Owl sees it," said Roo.

Tigger scratched his head. "Maybe you oughta just tell Owl—"

Roo shook his head. "He told me not to bounce on it, but I forgot. Now I have to fix it somehow."

Tigger turned to Owl. "Say, Owl," he said, "hope ya don't mind, but we're gonna take the stool down to show Pooh."

Before Owl could answer, Tigger scooped up Roo and the
stool. They bounced down the tree past a very surprised Pooh.
"See, here's the stool, Buddy Boy!" Tigger said to Pooh.

Tigger and Roo hurried away. They stopped to catch their
breath near Pooh's house.

"Look, Tigger!" Roo pointed to one of Pooh's honey pots.
"I bet we could fix that leg with some of Pooh's honey."

"Good thinkin', Roo Boy!" said Tigger. "Why, that honey oughta stick just like glue."

They carefully poured the honey onto the stool leg, but it didn't fix things. It just made the stool very sticky.

They bounced over to Rabbit's garden. "This'll work just fine!" Tigger called, pulling a bean vine from its pole.

Tigger wrapped the bean vine around the leg of the stool. It worked perfectly—until the vine snapped.

Roo couldn't take the stool back to Owl now. "Maybe we should try something else," he said in a small voice.

Tigger smacked himself on the head. "Hey, I know!" he said. "Ol' Long Ears has stringy beans in his garden! We'll use those!"

"Hmm," said Tigger. "Those musta been snap beans instead of string beans!"

"We'll just have to find something else," Roo said.

As they headed out of the garden, they ran into Eeyore.

"Say, can we borrow some thistles, Eeyore?" Roo asked.
"We need them to fix . . . something."

"Help yourself," said Eeyore.

But prickly and stickly as they were, the thistles wouldn't
stay wound around the stool leg.

"What'll I do now, Tigger?" Roo asked.

"C'mon, Bouncin' Buddy. We'll go see Christopher Robin.
Fixin' goopy what-what-what stools is what Christopher Robins
do best!" Tigger bounced away with Roo close behind.

Tigger and Roo found Christopher Robin at his house.
"Hello, Roo!" said Christopher Robin. "Hello, Tigger. I was
just on my way to see Owl's *Who's Who* stool."
Roo pointed at the stool. "Well, here it is," he said sadly.

"They'll be mad at me," Roo said.

"It's okay," said Christopher Robin. "They will understand once you tell them the whole story."

"C'mon, Roo," said Tigger. "I'll bounce home with ya."

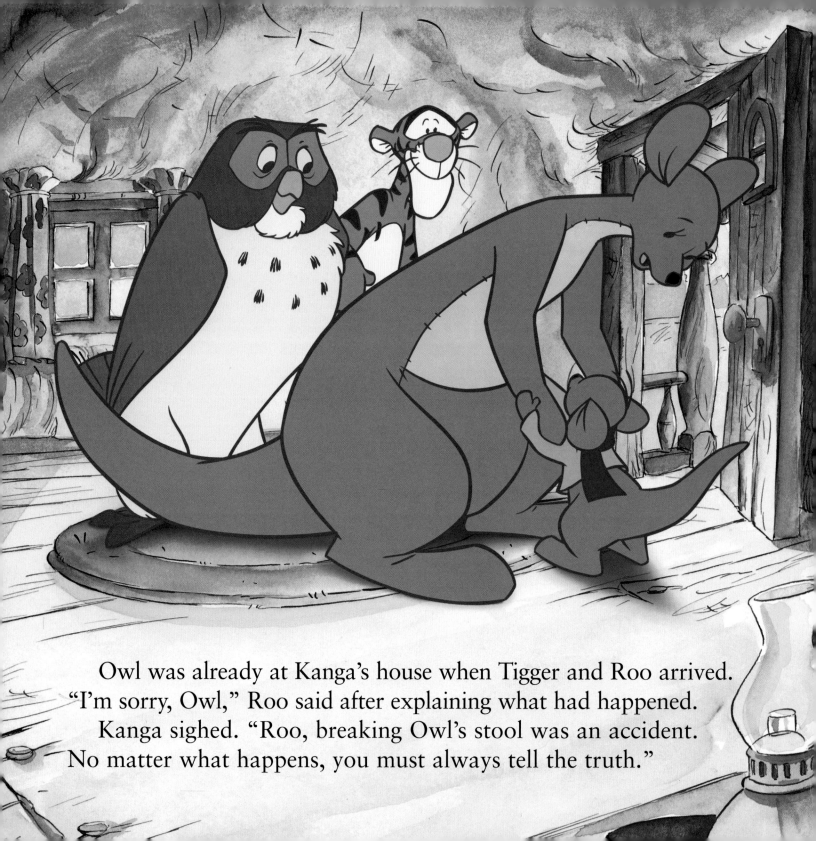

Owl was already at Kanga's house when Tigger and Roo arrived.
"I'm sorry, Owl," Roo said after explaining what had happened.
Kanga sighed. "Roo, breaking Owl's stool was an accident.
No matter what happens, you must always tell the truth."

"Yes, Mama," Roo said. He looked over at Owl, hoping that he wouldn't be angry.

"Perhaps I'll go check on that stool," said Owl as he turned to Roo. "Would you like to join me?"

"Sure," said Roo in a small voice.

Roo was relieved to see what a magnificent job Christopher Robin had done. The stool looked perfect.

A week later, Owl stood upon the mended *Who's Who* stool and read the names of all the owls who had done great things that year.

"Oh, my," said Christopher Robin. He looked at the honey and the bean vine and the thistle. "It's—"

"It's broken," said Roo. "And it's all my fault. Tigger helped me try to fix it, but I only made it worse."

"I haven't told Owl or my mama, either," Roo added.
Christopher Robin looked at the broken stool. "I think
I can fix this, Roo," he said. "But I also think you need to
tell them the truth."

Then Owl said, "And finally, there is our own Roo, who came forward and told the truth this year."

Roo was delighted when Owl read his name. "From now on, I'm gonna *always* tell the truth!" he cried.

A LESSON A DAY
POOH'S WAY

Telling the truth

puts the "bounce"

back in your step!